Tales from THE IRON TRIANGLE

For April & Dan a great young pair in Duck Cove Regards, Jim Polese

Tales from the

IRON TRIANGLE

Boyhood Days in the San Francisco

Bay Area of the 1920s

By James Polese

▲ ▲ ▲ ▲ ▲ ▲ ▲ ▲ ▲ ▲

OCEAN TREE BOOKS
San Francisco · Santa Fe · New Orleans

OCEAN TREE BOOKS
Post Office Box 1295
Santa Fe, New Mexico 87504
(505) 983-1412

Copyright © 1995 by James Polese
First Edition.
Printed in the United States of America
Cover design by Richard Polese
Drawings by Elizabeth Morales

International Standard Book Number: 0-943734-12-6

Library of Congress Cataloging in Publication data:

Polese, James, 1914—
    Tales from the Iron Triangle: boyhood days in the Bay Area of
the 1920s / by James Polese. — 1st ed.
    ISBN 0-943734-12-6 : $9.95
    1. Richmond (Calif.) — Social life and customs — Juvenile
literature. 2. Polese, James, 1914- —Childhood and youth—Juvenile
literature. 3. Richmond (Calif.)— Biography— Juvenile literature.
[1. Richmond (Calif.)—Social life and customs. 2. Polese, James, 1914-
—Childhood and youth.] I. Title
F869.R5P65 1994
979.4'63—dc20   94-22857
                                                          CIP AC

For my wife, Esther,

our children, and grandchildren

Tales from THE IRON TRIANGLE

Contents

Preface

THESE STORIES WERE WRITTEN in an attempt to capture and record in essence a way of life as it was lived by a certain segment of our American population in the early 1920s.

The neighborhood in which these tales take place, the Iron Triangle, was at the time a sparsely settled district on the northwest outskirts of the city of Richmond in the San Francisco Bay Area. The name comes from the convergence there of the Santa Fe and Southern Pacific railroad tracks.

The people for the most part were immigrant Italian families. Interspersed here and there were a family or two of Slavonian, German, Austrian, and African ancestry—as well as a few families that our parents referred to as "Americans."

Factories, mostly within walking distance, provided jobs for the men and a few of the women. Pasture lands for tethered animals and wild oat fields surrounded our homes. Nearby were baylands, creeks and truck farms—places of adventure and discovery for young boys of that bygone era.

"Conservation" and "recycling" were not common terms in those times, yet such values were practiced by these people of European background as they took advantage of the range of the natural and manmade resources the area offered. Their habits, ethics, and attitudes gave the community a certain level of cohesiveness, which extended to their children.

These tales from the Iron Triangle are based on factual experiences and conditions. I have taken a few liberties, however, to give them continuity and to hold the interest of young readers.

James Polese
Inverness, California
September 1994

Tales from the

IRON TRIANGLE

Ambrose

SOME SAY THAT YOUR INDIVIDUALITY is the product of your environment, the sum total of all your experiences. Others say that it is simply the result of your ancestral heredity. More than likely it's both. But it was not so in the case of Ambrose.

No, Ambrose was *Ambrose*. If I may venture a scientific or at least an educated guess, it would be that his character was the result of an accident of nature, perhaps a random something that altered the component parts of his embryonic chromosomes. Let me assure you, however, if it was such an accident, the results were not freakish.

No, indeed, Ambrose was a complete, complex character, but one not easily visualized by a few descriptive adjectives. Nor do I believe that he was affected much by his environment. Ambrose *was* the environment, and as such he affected all others about him. The many facets of his personality were so subtly and artistically patterned that they produced, in my mind, an everlasting gem of a human being.

The boy, Ambrose, ceased to exist when in his middle teens he changed his name to Frank. But that is getting ahead of my story. So let me start from the beginning—the day he moved in next door at the age of six in the summer of 1920.

My mother, who was a very frugal woman, did not believe in wasting anything, not even the productivity of child labor, and so I found myself, a six-year-old, cranking the family butter churn and developing both muscle and *character*, as mother would put it. I could tell from the sloshing and bumping inside the wooden churn that my tedious job was nearing its end when a sudden crash against the wall of our clapboard house startled us both.

"Well, I guess it's that new boy next door who probably wants to meet you. Go," she added, and untypically rewarded me with a small box of raisins.

Perhaps she wants me to share it with the boy, I thought.

Raisins in hand, I ripped down the back stairway, danced through a bean patch and then assaulted the board fence that separated our yards—the same fence from whence that clod of dirt was launched that so suddenly ended my labors.

Perched there on the fence I watched the new boy, who was not much bigger than I was, creeping along a flowering patch of potatoes. I started to say something like, What's your name? but he slowly raised his left hand as if to say *be quiet*. Then suddenly his right hand darted to a flower in which a honey bee was doing its thing. With a triumphant smile he held the struggling bee aloft by pinching its wings between thumb and forefinger. He approached me with it and, although I wasn't sure what he had in mind, I held my ground. He then extended his heavy cotton suspender strap to the bee's underbelly. The bee cooperated by driving his stinger deep into the fabric—which, of course, cost him his life, as bees cannot retract their stingers. With a quick jerk the boy detached the bee, leaving the stinger and a yellowish sticky glob of innards with it.

"My name is Ambrose—Am, for short," he said, stomping on the moribund insect. Mean, just plain mean, you might say, just like a guy who plucks a wing from a fly. I knew better. Yes, he had sacrificed that bee, but in so doing he calculatingly impressed upon me that he was brave, imaginative and quick. Ambrose certainly would be someone I would have to contend with in the future.

Well, not to be completely outdone, I deliberately opened my box of raisins and slowly selected a large one, tossed it high into the air and caught it in my mouth. I chewed it slowly, as though to savor its sweetness, and finally, with an audible smacking of my lips, swallowed it. I watched his throat as it swallowed after mine.

"My name's Jim," I said, noting now that he was fingering something bright in his hands.

"Dibs," he stated flatly, which in the parlance of boys in those days meant that he had laid claim to at least a portion of my raisins. I ignored the claim. "What you got there?" I asked.

"An Eversharp pencil—see, it's automatic," and he demonstrated its workings, but he did not allow me to touch it.

"I'll swap you for the raisins," he offered.

"Sure," I said, and after making the exchange, departed as fast as I had come, in order that I might relish my new prize in private. "Yeah, brave and quick," I said to myself, "but, gosh, how dumb—a brand new automatic pencil for a few lousy raisins!"

It wasn't long before I had to revise my appraisal as there came, that same afternoon, a knock on the back door. It was one of Ambrose's older sisters. She had Ambrose in tow, holding him by the back of his bib-overall suspenders, which had the effect of choking him if he resisted.

"I want my pencil," she said evenly.

"Nothing doing—it's mine! I traded for it fair and square!"

The girl's face started to contort as though she was going to cry, but a stern look directed at me from my mother, followed by a jerking nod of her head in the direction of the girl, settled the matter. I knew that I had been had.

"But I want my raisins back then," I said, trying to salvage something out of the unhappy affair.

"Sorry, but I et them," said Ambrose with a shrug. In defeat I turned and went to my room.

Boy, I'm sure going to get even some day—

That day was long in coming. Like I said, this was just the beginning.

A Boat Named Angie

THE PRICE OF SCRAP CAST IRON in 1926 was pegged at one cent per pound on location. At least that was the price offered by a certain scrap dealer.

Each Saturday morning the sonorous call of *"Rags-bones-bottles-sacks..."* would be heard over the meadows, which came from the old junk dealer as he swayed from side to side on his aged one-horse rig. His wagon creaked and its load rattled as it made its way slowly over the uneven dirt road.

At the call of "Hey, Junkie!" he would rein his horse at a boy's backyard and then would begin the long haggling over the price, quality and weight of the boy's collection of scrap copper, rags and the inevitable small heap of scrap cast iron. The transaction was generally concluded with, "My last offer and, so help me Got, I von't make a dime!"

The scrap iron represented the basic source of "spending money" for the little boys of this semi-rural and semi-industrial community. They "mined" the cast iron in the form of chips, risers and sprues from the sand tailings of a bathtub foundry that fringed their neighborhood and beyond which lay the tidal lands of South San Pablo Bay.

It was a particularly hot Saturday and the pickin's were rather lean at the tailings where Ambrose, Lou and I decided to pool our efforts. "Let's go swimmin'," suggested Ambrose who, as usual, soon became bored with the work.

"Okay," I agreed. "But let's get this stuff loaded on Lou's wagon first and we'll pick it up on the way back." Lou's "wagon" consisted of an unmatched set of baby buggy wheels, a lug box, a few boards and a minimum of hardware, mostly reclaimed nails.

It was ingeniously assembled in such a way that the front wheels could pivot.

We took a shortcut to the swimming hole, walking over the thick, springy pickleweed grass, sometimes tripping over the colorful hairy moss, and occasionally plunging suddenly into a hidden meandering waterway. Each misfortune brought good-natured guffaws and taunts from the others but, for the most part, our attention was on our surroundings—the sudden flurry of a startled clapper rail, the clucking of a coot or the plaintive cries of shore birds. We encountered the lesser of one of the two sloughs that eventually met with each other and whose tidal currents at times swirled at this convergence to form a deep sandy-bottomed swimming hole.

While we were resting at the edge of this slough, I noticed a half-submerged structure that lay eastward along the slough in a distant cove. *The prow of a small boat...* I thought. I said nothing—just glanced away—and although my heart was beating wildly, I said casually, "Hey guys, let's go!"

Westward and at the swimming hole we saw our friends Charley and Barney from North Richmond, a bordering community. This unincorporated area was the result of an abortive attempt by early and unregulated land developers who promotionally acclaimed "the Second Addition to the City of Richmond." Premature bronze plaques mounted on impressive monuments attested to the same. The two communities, which were separated physically by a railroad spur and to a certain degree socially, nevertheless retained a friendly, if somewhat reserved, relationship.

Charley, a sickly lad, was resting, but Barney was busily repairing a springboard which was constructed on a shell mound (undoubtedly once a Huchiun Indian midden) at the apex of the sloughs.

Off came bib-overalls, blue workshirts and BVDs—shoes were never worn in the summertime. We splashed into the cold water and swam and dove, even though none of us had ever had a lesson.

My heart just wasn't in it. I felt guilty about not sharing my secret and I was anxious to get away so that I could later return alone in order to fully appraise *my* discovery.

We were standing by a small driftwood fire drying off when, to my relief, Lou said, "I've got to head back and help my father with the irrigation."

"I'm going down the road aways with Barney and Charley," said Ambrose, thereby avoiding both the work of retrieving the cast iron and the sharing of the licorice whips he intended to buy at the little store on the longer way around.

I started back with my friend Lou and after a bit, "Hey, Lou, hold up, I got somethin' I want to..."

"Yes, I know," interrupted Lou, "I saw it, too."

Off we bounded over the pickleweed grass, running, falling, panting, and finally gasping as we looked over *our* boat. Without a word between us, we went to work in the mud and water, gradually working the boat partially up a bank, spilling out some of the water and splashing out most of the rest. Using the pickleweed moss, we scrubbed away the slime and muck.

When we inched her hourglass stern clear of the water, we could barely make out the weather-beaten painted scrawl—*ANGIE*.

"She looks good—just waterlogged," said Lou.

"I'll betcha we can sail her," I added with a grin, noting the mast stepping-hole in the forward thwart.

We hated to leave her, but we knew she would be safe there for awhile; the tides were moderate at the time as the moon was just a little over half full. We trudged back, overcome by our strenuous efforts and the enormity of our find. Silently, we pulled the cartload of cast iron to Lou's father's small part-time truck farm which adjoined the foundry.

We then went about our individual chores—Lou irrigating the vegetables and me feeding the two cows and filling the wood box. Although all of the men in this area had full-time jobs, almost all the families maintained a garden and chickens. Some had a cow, goats or rabbits, and occasionally a pig. My family had a big white horse, Ambrose's a bay, Lou's an unmatched pair of plough horses, and Mr. Sorenson, the drayage man, a pair of retired draft horses. There was always plenty to do!

On weekdays (which included Saturdays then) supper was at five-thirty, just one-half hour after the foundry's quitting time whistle. My final after-supper task was to deliver milk to the neighbors who did not have a cow or whose cows were "dry." Untypically, I looked forward to this task this evening, rearranging my route so that I would end up at Lou's place so that we could make plans for the boat.

I set my "empties" near the hand pump which was under the windmill and gave out with a soft two-fingered whistle call. Lou responded instantly and came bounding down the external back stairway of the two-story frame house. Most of the houses in the area were two stories; the lower story was usually an undivided, unpaved area which served as a wine cellar, milk house, workshop, and a get-together place for informal meetings.

It was here that we formulated our plans for *Angie*. We knew practically nothing of boating, let alone sailing. Our knowledge was mostly based upon experience or from observing others such as our older brothers or fathers. It did not occur to us to use the library and we had not even heard of bookstores. After considerable discussion, we finally concluded that we should bring Barney into the deal. At least Barney had spent a summer at "South Solito" across the bay with an uncle of his who was a fisherman. We also agreed that secrecy was essential as we were not sure that the "losers-weepers, finders-keepers" law was respected by adults.

Lou and I couldn't wait, so we ran over to Barney's, slowing down as we approached his house to catch our breath so as not to arouse suspicion from Barney's mother. Barney, who was a bit older, a bit of a loner, and not really regarded as part of "the gang," reacted well to our proposal.

"You'll need a mast, a boom, a sail, a halyard, a sheet, a rudder and a tiller to get her sailing," he said. "Maybe some cotton if we have to caulk any open seams."

Lou and I were impressed with all the new terms that Barney used and were elated with his seemingly endless wealth of boating knowledge.

"Okay," said Barney with finality, and savoring his new-found leadership, "I'll tell you what—we'll look her over tomorra' after church, and we'll see what's what."

Lou and I dutifully endured the long period of kneeling at mass this particular Sunday morning, and we perfunctorily murmured the "Our Fathers" and "Hail Marys." After making excuses to Ambrose's suggestion of, "Hey, let's play two-a-cat," we high-tailed it home.

Sunday afternoon was one's own free time, but it was also the custom in our neighborhood that the most bountiful of all meals was served at two o'clock, which was still several hours off.

"Well, I'm just going to have to tell Ma and Pa," I thought as I kicked off my Sunday shoes and corduroy knee pants, and slipped into my bib-overalls.

My house was one of the few that had an internal stairway and at this time it resounded with the melodic *aria* of *"La Dona e Mobile."* My dad, although a proud, hardworking and energetic man, was also very cheerful. His voice was strong and expressive, and he had a great singing range. He usually led the Italian men in songfests when they gathered in one of the basement "cantinas" during festive occasions.

I waited respectfully while watching my father put the finishing touches on a cooper's adze handle which he had fashioned from an oak wagon spoke. He sure can do anything with tools, I thought admiringly. I realized that my presence was acknowledged when my father slipped his singing into his native *Friulano* version of *"Cheri beri bin"* and directed the endearing words to me, his youngest son. We both laughed before he could finish.

"What ees it, Jeem?" questioned father, who unlike my mother often spoke to his children in English. He was so proud of his adopted country.

"Pa, we found a boat—Lou and I—and it is beautiful—just beautiful."

"A boat? A boat?" questioned father, and shaking his head, "We know nothing of boats..." Then changing his expression he said, "...but you will learn."

"Go," he said finally, "but be careful—and take some bread and cheese."

I bounded up the stairs to comply, but was met by my mother who had overheard the remarks. She handed me the heel section of still warm, home-baked bread and a piece of cheese with the usual parting admonition of, "*Fa bravo, Gino*" (Be good, Jim).

As I ran through the backyard, I reached down into the quarter loaf and extracted the soft part of the bread which I tossed into the chicken yard. The cheese I inserted into the hollowed crust and slipped it in the commodious back pocket of my bibbed overalls.

It didn't take me long to converge with the other boys and I noticed that Barney was carrying a gunnysack.

Lou and I watched Barney intently as he went about examining the boat, probing here and there for dry rot with his pocket knife.

"She's good, she's sound! I'll nail that loose plank on her transom while you guys clean her up," he said, taking some tools from the sack.

By the time Lou and I had finished our task, Barney had the loose plank nailed back into position and had caulked its seams with cotton. Without ceremony, we re-launched her and she floated true on her waterline. We waded alongside of her, meaning to scramble aboard, when we remembered we had no oars. We scrounged the bank for driftwood and each selected what he thought would substitute for a paddle, and this time we boarded her from an overhanging bank.

We paddled hard but made slow progress. It didn't take us long to realize that we were bucking the current. Reversing our course, we were soon moving along peacefully. Barney directed us into a small inlet. I pulled out my bread and cheese and we sat on the bank munching it and admiring *Angie* as we made plans for rigging her.

"She ought to sail okay," said Barney. "She's got good lines and a deep skeg. I kin make a sail from one of my mom's old sheets." (Sheets were made of heavy, coarse cotton in those days.) "Marconi rig and loose-footed would be the easiest," he continued, "I think I've got sumpin' I kin use for a boom, but how about a mast?"

"'Member that big ol' white house that burnt down two years ago?" questioned Lou. "I swiped its flagpole and I've still got it."

"Great," said Barney, and taking a ball of string from his sack, he stretched it the length of the boat and then added a few more feet before cutting it off.

"Look, Lou, this is the length we need and she's gotta be smaller that this here hole," he said, tying a knot near the end of the string, indicating the diameter.

Barney then took a stick and drew the shape of the rudder and tiller, full-scale, on an exposed area of mud. Both he and Lou had confidence in my skill with tools and knew that I could be trusted with this important task. Having divided the work, Barney said that he would be ready in a few days and we all agreed to meet at the boat Wednesday morning.

I went right to work on the family scrap wood pile and selected the material I needed. The rudder would have to be made from several pieces (the plywood industry was still in its infancy). I squared the edges and drilled and doweled. I applied glue from a heated glue pot. Not having large enough clamps, I laid the assembly on the bench and forced the boards together with wedges, just as I had seen my father do. By the next day the glue had dried and I shaped the rudder with a saw, plane and rasp.

That evening my father brought me a pair of old brass door hinges to serve as gudgeons and pintals. In my enthusiasm, I left the plane face downward on the bench. My dad did not scold me; he merely, but pointedly, laid it on its side. He knew that I would not forget again.

We then dumped the "hell box" of salvaged nuts and bolts and the two of us selected the most appropriate ones for mounting the hinges. That done, my father placed a pair of slats across the grain of the rudder. I got the idea of the needed reinforcement and the next day I had them glued and screwed down in place.

And now for the tiller! Of course, an ever-useful wagon wheel spoke would do fine. I shaped it and that evening my father helped me mount it on the rudder. It was ready—and tomorrow was Wednesday!

We boys met at the swimming hole and together hauled and tugged our gear to the boat.

But there was no boat! We looked at each other in silent dismay, until we heard the mischievous chuckle of Ambrose, that irrepressible prankster.

"Dang!" said Lou, who did not swear.

"Damn!" said I, who did at times.

"Have a jelly bean," said Ambrose, emerging from his hiding place. "Cut me in and I'll tell ya where 'tis."

Lou, ignoring the sweets and with clenched fist, countered in a deliberate and firm voice, "*You-can-come-as-a-pass-en-ger.* Now, square up and get to work!" he growled. We boys worked diligently. We had trouble stepping the mast, but after several tries we managed it and wedged it into place. The mounting of the rudder went well and we had the boom swinging on an improvised gooseneck. We scrambled aboard and Barney raised the sail.

"Take the tiller, Jim, and I'll handle the sheet, and *sit down, Am!*" ordered Barney. Lou was up at the bow with a slender pole, helping to get the boat clear and underway.

The sail filled and we were soon moving! We thrilled in the silent departure. Soon we arrived at the swimming hole and I threw the tiller over so as to enter the converging slough. The wind caught the other side of the sail and suddenly the boom started swinging over.

"Sit down, Am..!" Barney started to yell, but it was too late. There was a dull thud as the boom caught Ambrose on the head and catapulted him into the water.

"Serves him right," muttered Lou, as Barney dropped the sail. By paddling and poling we got back to Ambrose, whose greatest injury was that to his dignity—which he tried to hide with a sheepish grin.

"Guess we'd better stow it for today," said Barney, as he threw Ambrose a hemp line and told him to pull us back to our berth. On the way in, Barney explained the need for the helmsman to call out, *"Ready about"* or *"Helms-a-lee."*

"Let's go down the big slough tomorra'," I suggested. "We kin get in some practice sailing. It widens out, ya know!"

The next morning all four of us, with our lunches packed, met at the boat. A light, fair wind was blowing and we were off. We managed the swimming hole turn with a controlled jibe and glided into the larger slough.

We soon passed a group of hunter and fishermen shacks with rickety wharves. These shacks could be reached by a very rudimentary dirt road, except at flood tides. We subconsciously noticed the direction that smoke blew from a tin chimney of one of the shacks. It was occupied by old Dan Bailey who lived a hermit-like existence there. He waved to us from his doorway as we went by.

We sailed on, taking turns at the tiller and at handling the sheet. A lookout was posted forward. We were already munching on our lunches when Barney, who was on lookout, whispered, "Look ahead, *sea lions!*"

Lou eased the sheet and the boat slowed to a glide. We boys were fascinated by a harbor seal and her pup who were peering at us from a muddy bank. Slithering into the water, the seals continued to watch us curiously as the boat went by.

We sailed on, quietly observing the various shore birds, pointing out to each other some of the unique features of each— such as the down-turned bill of the curlew or the upturned one of the avocet. We were particularly amused at the nodding and teetering of the sandpipers. Except for the killdeer, which sometimes frequented our meadows, not knowing their names we called all shore birds "snipes."

The ever-widening slough gave us room to maneuver and we sailed to all points of the compass, including tacking to windward. Occasionally we would startle small groups of ducks or cause a solitary grebe to dive. We delighted in being the first to spot the emerging bird.

Now we were peacefully running with wind and into fairly open water. I looked westward at the Standard Oil storage tanks that nestled in the far hillside and chuckled as I recalled that as a very small boy, seeing these white tanks in the distance from my home, thought they were cheeses—just like the cheese my mother was curing on the long high shelves in our basement. My reflections soon turned to concern as the afternoon wind, which had been freshening, began kicking up some whitecaps.

We realized that we had to turn back and so we came about and headed back to the channel. Now heading windward, we started some long tacks. We were heeling at a fairly steep angle and the boat started to ship water. Lou and Ambrose began to bail furiously as the wind picked up. Barney glanced at the distant shoreline with each tack and realized that we were making very little progress.

"We must be bucking a pretty good current," said Barney who was at the tiller, adding ruefully, "Next time, we'll figure on tides and currents, or at least we had better bring along something for an anchor—then we could stay put until the current slacked."

There might not *be* a next time, I thought, but I knew it was no good saying so. Instead: "Remember that channel marker? Think that we can reach it, guys?"

"Let's give it a try," shouted Lou.

We struggled feverishly with sail, paddles and bailers—and finally, near exhaustion, we found the stick that was driven into the mud by some fisherman to indicate the channel. Ambrose slung a line around it and we hoped the stick would hold. It did, but it bent dangerously with the added pressure.

"Let 'er go!" I yelled. *"Let-her-go!"*

Ambrose slipped the line while I made a loop on the other end of the tether, weighting it with a hammer and whatever bits of metal I could find. Of course, the other boys soon realized what I was up to. Surely the stick would hold if we could get the loop over and down the stick. Ambrose threw the loop over it. The loop

sank rapidly as I played out all of the line. Intuitively I knew that the more "scope" it had the better.

Being satisfied with the results, we dropped our sail and hunched down into a huddle, wrapping the sail around us to protect us from the wind. It had started as a long wait, but as our bodies warmed, we were soon exchanging stories and "remember whens," reliving some of our earlier misadventures.

We knew that after the current slackened we would make it back, but we started to become apprehensive as the sun began to lower against the skyline of Mount Tamalpais ("the sleeping woman").

The wind was abating when I thought that I could hear the steady *chug-chug-chug* of machinery. Peering out from over the sail I saw the clipper bow of a Monterey fishing boat pushing a bow wave in our direction.

Without killing her old Hicks "one lunger" engine, her skipper brought her slowly alongside. We boys secured the boats both fore and aft and retrieved our tethering line.

"Ho-kay, fine, boys," bellowed the skipper in a low, gravelly, but friendly voice. "Come aboard."

I recognized the voice. It belonged to the suntanned Slavonian fishmonger who made his rounds every Friday morning at my neighborhood to sell his catch. Money seldom exchanged hands when he stopped a my house. Instead, fish, clams or crabs were exchanged for butter, eggs or cheese. There was no bartering—in fact, the fisherman and my mother would try to outdo each other in their generosity. The generosity of one was always protested by the other, but was invariably accepted.

"How is your mama, Gino? Will she have some *ricotta* for me Friday? Eh, Ambrose, your papa, has he won the horseshoe *tornamento*?" He did not wait for an answer, just kept saying things like, "Your mama, Barney, she is very strong. Best crate-maker at the tub factory and more faster than the men."

It was during this monologue that I noticed the lettering on a life ring: *A-N-G-E-L-I-N-A*.

"Here, Gino, take *Angelina*'s wheel. I want to look over her little Angie."

I was frightened, not so much of the wheel which I soon got the hang of, but of the fact that *Angie* had found her real owner and that we were going to lose her.

"Who find *Angie*?" Shes'a been gone a long time. She was my net boat when people eat smelt and herring. They just want line and hook fish now, like cod and salmon."

"Who find *Angie*?" he repeated and this time he looked at each boy and waited for an answer. Lou and I nodded guiltily.

"Well," the man said slowly. "I don't need her very much anymore. Old Dan Bailey soma-time. Ah, we be partners, Gino, Luigi, Dan and me. We keep her at Dannie's and you boys paint her up good. Ol' Dan, he learn you many things—how to fish and how to splice and tie plenty knots. You use *Angie* any time. Ho-kay?" he asked with a wink.

We were all smiling as the *Angelina*'s master took over the wheel to dock her at Dan Bailey's place. There on the dock was my father, who had stopped by after delivering a wine barrel in which he had replaced a couple of bad staves.

"*Eh, come va Gigi?*" (How are you), the Slavonian asked of my dad in Italian. Almost all *Triestinos* spoke both languages.

"Well, I thought I'd drop by just in case, you know, just in case."

The men drank the customary glass of wine and the boys piled into the wagon. My father picked up Old Prince's reins and eased himself onto the buckboard. I joined him and as we were leaving, the fisherman tossed a couple of salmon aboard. My father took the boys to their respective homes, giving each a half of salmon.

I helped father unhitch the big white horse, and then there followed a strange custom. Prince lowered his head and I locked my arms around his neck. Prince obligingly gave me a lift or two before extending his tether to nibble on some choice wild oats.

I was in bed and almost asleep when my door slowly opened. "Gino," my father said quietly in almost a whisper, "*Angie*, she is, how-you-say? *Be-oo-ti-ful.*"

Fear

"WE HAVE NOTHING TO FEAR but fear itself."

These words were spoken by my father one Halloween Eve at least twenty years before President Franklin Roosevelt immortalized them in his stirring address to our nation in its time of crisis. We had no radio or television in those days, but we were very fortunate that my father was an accomplished storyteller. He often provided us and our guests with lively entertainment.

One such occasion was a certain Halloween when some of my young friends and I were gathered in the darkness of our barn planning our evil doings. There were no "trick-or-treats" then—only tricks. Just the year before my father had suffered the inconvenience of retrieving our elegant, if outmoded, two-seat black-leathered surrey which mysteriously appeared on the rooftop of the streetcar terminus waiting-room.

Our scheming that night was interrupted by a strange moving light that sifted through the cracks and knotholes of the old barn. A stronger shaft of light soon descended upon us as its source approached the slit of the huge door that was partially ajar. With a groan-like noise, the door slowly swung open and, as our eyes adjusted to the light, the imposing figure of my father took form. He stood there holding a lantern in one hand while he solemnly twisted his moustache with the other. He stepped forward among us and silently examined our faces one by one.

Suddenly his demeanor changed and his smile exposed the friendly man that he was.

"Boys, have you ever heard of the mysterious St. Elmo's fire?" he asked as he hung the lantern on a harness peg.

Here it comes, I thought, another story. And what a story it was! His delivery in the faltering light of the kerosene lantern was not only dramatic, it was effective! He had us all plain scared by the time he was through. Sensing this, he attempted to ease our feelings with the old adage that I first referred to, but the result was a rather subdued Halloween.

It was just a day or so later that my father (who had been a vintner by trade) made his yearly announcement. He would soon realize his lifelong ambition, he said. He had made a deposit on a lovely vineyard in Calistoga and all that was needed to fulfill his dream was my mother's approval. He then proposed, since all of my older brothers and sisters were grown and gone from the house, that I should remain at home to take care of the barnyard animals while they made the overnight journey to Calistoga.

On this clear, cold night the wind could be heard whistling by the eaves of our two-story frame farmhouse. For the first time in my life, I was alone at night. I turned in early, seeking the warmth and safety of my bed. With my eyes closed, I chanted my prayers for comfort, but sleep would not come. I decided to get a glass of milk, but as I opened my eyes I saw a figure hovering over my brother's now-empty bed. It was with great relief that I finally realized that it was only my shirt hanging on the bedpost, dimly highlighted by the moonlight streaming through the lace-curtained windows.

The milk did made me feel better, but I still felt a bit apprehensive when a gust of wind made our old double-hung windows shudder. Returning to my room from the kitchen, and just as I turned off from the lighted hallway to enter my room, I saw a figure crossing the glass-paneled front door. I crouched by the wall of my room and thought I heard the front door rattle!

That's not the wind, I said to myself as I quickly peeked around the corner. The head in the glass panel of the door did the same! I dropped to my hands and knees and, very slowly, looked again. I saw the head clearly this time. It was *mine,* reflected in the window glass.

How foolish, how utterly foolish. Wasn't I ever going to grow up?

I turned off the hall light and returned to bed. After delivering a long self-deprecating harangue, I started to drop off to sleep when I heard—definitely and without a doubt—*footsteps* from the pantry just off the kitchen. The footsteps were very slow and deliberate, clear—even loud—as they progressed through the kitchen and into the hallway. A long pause at my open doorway and then "it" *entered!*

"Holy Mary, Mother of God, pray for us sinners..."

A step toward me!

"Now and at the hour..."

Another step!

"...of our death."

Don't move—hold your breath.

A step beside me!

I couldn't breathe—I couldn't scream—I blacked out!

The moon was replaced by a bright sun and it was shining in my eyes. I rubbed them, yawned and stretched—until I remembered that awful nightmare. No, it was not a dream. It was much too real. My leg reached over the edge of the bed in order to arise and dress, but instead of the usual cold floor, my foot sensed a soft something.

There "it" was—*dead!*

It was just a mouse that had one foot caught in a mousetrap. Dead. Frightened to death, I'm sure.

Yes, old Pop was right— "Often there is nothing to fear but fear itself."

The vineyard?

Well, mother would never leave her beloved neighborhood. And Dad, oh yes, he would try again—next year.

Friends

THE MANNER IN WHICH A MAN stacks his hay can often be traced to his national origin, and in some cases even to the particular province from which he emigrated. My father, however, having been a much-traveled man, was much more cosmopolitan in habit and so his haystacks reflected his individualism.

They had the form and grace of a teardrop whose point pierced still another teardrop of a smaller size. Architecturally they might be compared to the Byzantine or onion-like domes that graced the old cathedrals of Moscow. Artistic as they may have been, his designs were primarily practical, as the hay remained sweet the winter long and it was never tainted with mildew.

The winter of 1926 was one of heavy rains and the wild oats were tall and heavy with seed by hay time in late spring. The normally abundant California poppies had given up the struggle to outreach the overshadowing wild oats. The fresh-cut grass had cured well in the breezy, sunny days of late May. With the help of our horse Prince it was all hauled home by early June. It was dumped as a great circle of loose hay ready for stacking.

Inside this circle my father had built an open wooden platform about a foot high and sixteen feet in diameter. This was done in order to keep the hay off the ground and to provide the necessary ventilation. In its center stood a tall, slender pole.

With the help of several neighbors, hay was pitched onto the platform while we children interlaced it radially by patting it with a fork or a rake. As we worked we stomped the hay in a circular progression. Each layer became greater in diameter until the stack had reached its maximum girth.

When this height was reached, which was just about as high as a man could comfortably pitch a forkfull of hay, a temporary platform was built alongside the growing stack. The hay was then pitched to a man on the platform and he in turn relayed it up and onto the stack. The layers of hay were now gradually reduced in diameter as the stack grew. When the stack had reached within a few feet of the top of the pointed pole, we children slid down, with help from a rope that was tied to the pole, whereupon we were replaced on the stack by two men.

A large ball of hay was then prepared by rolling, patting and combing. It was secured with a rope and then hauled up to the top of the stack. The two men raised it over and onto the pointed pole. The men then descended by way of the rope.

Next came the combing and shaping of the stack's surface, which was done with a pitchfork and a long-handled rake. The combing effectively aligned the outermost hay like that of a thatched roof used for shedding the rain.

The remaining hay was piled onto the temporary platform and it was scheduled for first usage. A makeshift corral was then built around the main stack of hay.

The hot work was over and we knew that our blistered hands would soon heal. The good feeling of work well done prevailed and the Sunday dinner that awaited us was laced with good-natured banter.

▲ ▲ ▲

Sitting back on the porch while settling my dinner, I watched Old Bob, our mongrel dog, furiously digging in the garden. I don't know what his ancestral makeup was—surely some shepherd and some retriever was obvious—but where he inherited the life-long ambition to dig up a gopher was beyond me. Day in and day out he worked at this project with such determination that I am sure the garden suffered more from this activity than the damage a dozen gophers could have done.

I was watering the garden one day and Old Bob was excavating as usual when I thought that perhaps I could help him out by running the water down the gopher hole.

Help him I did! A dripping, gasping gopher emerged. Old Bob just stood there transfixed—and did absolutely nothing except stare at the quarry that had eluded him for so many years. The gopher began to show signs of recovery, but Old Bob was immobile. I couldn't figure out what was going on inside of that dog, and I was finally forced to dispatch the pitiful creature with a garden spade.

Old Bob was never known to dig for a gopher again. He became listless and bored in the months that followed. The coming of winter, however, brought a change in him when he found a new and consuming interest. This is how it came about:

The Slavonian fisherman, of whom I spoke earlier, had given my mother a semi-wild mallard duck, which because of a broken wing and a bad limp had spent the previous year near his cabin by the bayland slough. She did not seem to be accepted by the rest of her kind in their wire enclosure, but she did partake of the ground corn and the chopped greens that mother fed her ducks.

We never named the birds or animals that were sooner or later scheduled for the stew pot, but this duck was something a bit special. La Dauxa, we called her—which was simply an Italianized word for "the duck" (the spelling being my own). When the other ducks were laying eggs, my mother would gather them and place them under a setting hen. This she did, since a big Rhode Island Red hen could set a larger brood. Efficient as this system was, the ducklings, of course, could never identify with their real mothers.

When La Dauxa's time for laying came, she seemed even more estranged from her kind than ever. Our fowl were always let out during the day so that they could forage a bit for themselves. They were called in at evening for their feed and locked up in their protective enclosure. La Dauxa ranged further and further as the days wore on, and on several occasions she did not return for her evening meal and the protection of the enclosure. La Dauxa then disappeared completely.

Although my father had adapted well to the ways of this new country, he unconsciously held to certain European customs. The responsibility of all male daily chores fell upon the oldest son. This son would assign certain tasks to his younger brothers and he in turn would look after them—sort of a substitute father. So it was that Andy, my brother, would milk the cows, but to me he assigned suck tasks as preparing the cows for milking. This included currying and feeding, and washing their bags and teats with warm water. I accepted the situation and even looked forward to the evening regimen.

Andy was a great whistler and he had inherited my father's ability to sing. The sound of milk spurting into the pail was timed to his music. It was interrupted only by the mewing of our cat and her kittens as they waited impatiently for that unerring spurt of warm milk in their faces that Andy delivered without missing a beat.

Instead of using the excess hay that was piled on the temporary platform, I had been pulling hay from the lower reaches of the main stack. (We did not use a hay saw as that would have defeated the purpose of my father's design.) I improvised a ladder to the platform and had burrowed into the hay. This provided me with the equivalent of a snug tree-house, in which I spent many hours reading or just observing the killdeer in the meadows, or watching the winter rains.

It was from this perch that I was listening to Andy's evening milk concert when I saw La Dauxa proudly waddling through the grass towards us, with family in tow. Old Bob was filled with excitement but La Dauxa would have no part of him and chose the underside of the haystack to raise her brood. It was then that both he and I noticed the late arrival that was struggling through the grass—a skinny runt of a duckling.

Old Bob whined like a puppy and using his only means of expressing the tender care that welled within him, he licked the exhausted duckling into a wet, shivering ball.

I called my mother, who always seemed to have a way with small creatures. When she brought it into the house the duckling appeared near death. It could not even hold up its own head. Mother blew rhythmic short bursts of air into its beak and it began to revive. In the meantime, Old Bob was making a fuss at the kitchen door, pawing, scratching and whining to be let in. Mother made a bed from an old blanket and placed it in back of the kitchen stove. Contrary to house rules, Old Bob was allowed to curl up there that evening. *Il Dauxine* (the diminutive male form of La Dauxa in our dialect) snuggled down into the folds of his fur.

Little Dauxine responded to this special care, and after a few days he, much to Old Bob's concern, was reintroduced to his mother and siblings. It didn't work. Rejected by his own mother —an outcast.

My mother then thoughtfully relegated both Dauxine and Old Bob to the garden. Here they were happy. Downey Dauxine and his furry surrogate mother became inseparable. Dauxine prospered and became lean and strong on his diet of cabbage leaves and snails. For awhile Old Bob seemed young again and became ever more alert with his watchdog duties. Dauxine developed into a fine, colorful drake and mother did not clip his wings as she had but to call Old Bob and Dauxine would follow him in. They began to roam the neighborhood and one was never seen without the other.

Fully feathered by now, the drake began trying his wings, but Old Bob's health began to fail and he could no longer keep up with his friend. Old Bob was examined by the young veterinarian who had come to vaccinate our cows. We all met the verdict stoically: that it would be better to end his days mercifully, rather than prolong his suffering.

▲ ▲ ▲

It pains me even now to write the end of this story. We brothers took our dog to a high embankment of a distant creek. There, amongst the willows, my brother shot Old Bob in the head with a small caliber rifle. The dog dropped soundlessly, and we buried him in a shallow grave. We covered his body with sand and leaves.

Several days later Andy and I were playing catch-ball when we saw a dirty, limping dog approach us. Old Bob wagged his tail and licked our hands. We were hugging Old Bob when our father saw us. With understanding he gently touched us with his hands and then carried our faithful old dog to his final end.

I could not finish that wordless supper that evening. I ran to the privacy of my hayloft. There I cried uncontrollably. And then I cried again. That night Andy did not chide me for encroaching upon his side of the large bed that we shared.

Dauxine was now alone and friendless. He became restless when the wild geese and ducks began winging their way southward.

He joined them.

Ambrose the Trickster

THE PROLIFERATION OF THE COMIC BOOK phenomenon in the United States first occurred in 1922. It was introduced by an enterprising young man by the name of Ambrose, at the age of eight.

Living in a land that was practically devoid of periodicals and magazines, Ambrose realized the circulation potential that he could achieve amongst his peers. By scrounging through the downtown area trash bins (he always seemed to have free time to roam far and wide), Ambrose collected the *San Francisco Sunday Examiner* colored comics for a period of weeks. He then cut the "funnies" into strips and pasted them together on the left edge to form a book. These he rolled into a wad and bound them with a rubber band.

Shrewdly, he never sold them or swapped them outright. He only leased them for a day or less, which meant that he could re-lease them time and time again. Yes, Mutt and Jeff and the Katzenjammer Kids were a controlled market in our area—that is, until we discovered his resources. In the meantime, however, he managed to amass a treasure of wheels, hoops, marbles, and tops, which, by playing the market right, he eventually parlayed into further fortunes such as handballs and even a baseball mitt.

Ambrose was an affable, good looking lad. His boyish face had an ever-ready smile with which he invariably disarmed the uninitiated. He was not by any means the brightest boy in our second grade class, but somehow he made things happen. If one was bored, he had but to be in his company for a short while before becoming involved with him—which was sometimes more than one had bargained for.

One day after school had let out, he and I discovered, like most second graders the world over, that by pressing a thumb over

a drinking fountain we could momentarily increase the water pressure. With the same thumb and a bit of practice we could spurt water twenty feet or so with unerring accuracy. We teamed up on the late stragglers from the classrooms as they emerged from the door. More than likely teacher's pets, we thought, and therefore fair game.

Unfortunately, Miss Pemberton came out to investigate the ruckus and we unwittingly caught her in our crossfire. I froze in disbelief. I was mortified and remorseful as the austere but dripping-wet schoolmarm held me by the ear. Corporal punishment was meted out on the spot. I was made to extend my hand, palm down. The hard whack across my knuckles with a long pencil made me wince. I thought that my punishment was justified until I received a second whack. That one was for Ambrose in absentia whose quick reaction had allowed him to escape. I was a slow learner.

My path home and the awaiting woodpile that forever needed chopping led me across the high railroad grade that separated our community from the rest of the town. I was still rubbing my knuckles when I caught up with Ambrose, who couldn't cross the tracks as a long train of freight cars was slowly passing, approaching the nearby switching yards.

From my position below I then saw him mount a car by its steel ladder. He scaled the car nearly to its top and then, reaching through the slats, he appeared to be helping himself to its contents. This was a fruit car and it was constructed like a lettuce crate to provide the necessary ventilation, as this was before the days of refrigerated cars.

It was peach season and Ambrose had his shirt bulging with fruit. He prepared to dismount the car just like an experienced brakeman might. With one foot on the lowest rung of the ladder and the other one poised for the necessary sprint, he swung out and made his descent. But he misjudged the weight the fruit had upon his center of gravity and he tumbled head-over-heels, squashing some of the peaches against his body and spilling the rest down the embankment.

I laughed and was enjoying those peaches when I realized

that I was the target of a barrage of missiles from above.

"Them's my peaches!" he yelled. But before I could respond, I caught a piece of two-inch railroad ballast on the top of my head which laid me low.

I had staggered halfway home before I regained full consciousness. It was not Ambrose but a young railroad bum that was steadying my course. He had his old, red handkerchief about my neck to catch the flow of blood as it dripped from my head. He had witnessed the whole affair.

"Where do you live, sonny?" he asked, and I pointed to our home. Mother met us as we entered the back yard. The two attended to my wound without talking; the man operating the hand pump at the well while she washed and then dried me with a pillow case plucked from the clothesline. My wound, they decided, was superficial and my mother applied her antiseptic solution of garlic juice.

Mother had thanked him in her best English and he was about to take his leave when his face lifted and his nostrils dilated. He had caught the scent of the bread that was baking in our outdoor oven—which mingled with the odor of fresh coffee roasting in a separate compartment of the same source.

Without a word he picked up the double-bladed ax and went right to work on the wood pile. My, how he did work! He stopped only from time to time to wipe the perspiration from his face.

Mother then realized who my benefactor was—a hungry bum. By the time she had assembled some sausage, cheese and bread and ground some fresh roasted coffee, my friend had split a huge pile of wood. The splitting of firewood was normally my chore, but thanks to Ambrose I now had at least a month's supply. I was just plain lucky, and realizing it I was determined to keep my guard high if I were to survive.

It was not that Ambrose was always able to avoid punishment or retribution for his transgressions. That did not seem terribly important to him; besides, he often managed to victimize his punisher in the process.

I suppose that even his father, who was a temperate man, was pushed to the limit of his patience. What caused him to resort to the use of the whip one day I never knew, but it only happened once.

We were having a quiet supper one evening when the peace of the neighborhood was shattered by the anguished screams of a poor little boy being beaten to death. My parents, who never used even the slightest slap to teach us right from wrong, were aghast as the screaming continued. My mother reacted by slamming the screen door again and again. Then all was suddenly quiet. Only I knew that Ambrose had exaggerated the pain and suffering—to shame his father, of course. His father could not risk a reputation as a child beater. Ambrose had seen to that.

My suspicions were verified the next day at the swimming hole. Ambrose's stark naked body did not have a mark on it.

The Bootleggers

ANDY'S VOICE PUNCTURED my concentration. I was resoling a pair of my work shoes with some discarded leather belting which had been used to drive a compressor at an ice-manufacturing plant nearby.

"Hey Jim, hitch up Old Prince. We've got to go over to San Pablo with the wagon," said my older brother. I sensed resentment in his voice. I knew he had planned on playing baseball that Saturday morning. My father had instructed him regarding the chores he wanted us to do that day and they didn't include baseball.

I retrieved our tethered big white horse from the field, slipped on his collar, hanes, belly band, and traces, and backed him into the wagon shafts. This was no trouble for me as Prince was always very cooperative. Andy checked out my work, then gave the belly band an extra tug.

"Guess we'd better replace those trace straps some day—leather's getting old and cracked," he remarked as he replaced Prince's halter with bridle and reins.

We traveled north, past the monument that marked the limits of the "Second Addition to the City of Richmond," then onto a dirt road that led us past the *cough-cough-chug-chug* sound of a water pumping station. Soon we were into the willow trees and over a wooden bridge that spanned San Pablo Creek.

Emerging through more willows, we continued on the road past several truck farms that often employed us neighborhood children in such tasks as picking beans, potatoes, tomatoes, planting onion sets, or even repairing lettuce crates.

We stopped at my father's friend, Serafino's, for some unmarketable greens for our cows, rabbits and chickens, and started back.

"Serafino is sure a nice guy," I remarked to Andy. "He brings us a new wool shirt or a ten-dollar gold piece every Christmas."

"Oh sure," was his response. "He's got five kids, all girls, and he sees us as good hard-working sons-in-law. Enough said?"

Then, "Look over there—" Andy had spotted an old onion field that was overgrown with a thick layer of morning glory. We figured that it might be good feed for our cows, so we cut out squares of this weed, rolled it into manageable bundles and hoisted them onto the wagon. This made for a heavy load, so we decided to skip the cutting of a few faggots of willow fronds that our mother wanted for bean poles.

We were on the road through the willows and were crossing the creek bridge when we noticed a lug box with some strange gadgets on it. We were about to stop to investigate the contraption when two masked men came shouting out of the woods.

They were trying to mount our wagon! Andy, with his own shout, whipped our horse and Prince took off in terror. We were so busy just hanging on over this rough road that we did not notice that the men had given up their chase.

Less than a quarter of a mile down the road one of Prince's harness traces broke, causing the single tree of the wagon to strike his hind legs with each stride, which drove him faster still.

Suddenly I felt myself flying through the air just as our wagon hit a large bump. Andy and I found ourselves sitting by the side of the road. The wheels of our overturned wagon were still idly turning and our horse was gone.

Our father met us as we straggled back toward home. We eagerly told him about our experience, but his only comment was, "*Bruti bestie* (dirty beasts)..." I did hear him mumble something about "bootleggers," but he did not enlarge on it. We kids were concerned about the horse and wagon.

"Prince come home bye'n bye and I feex the wagon," our father said reassuringly. He seemed preoccupied with other thoughts. The next day we found out why.

My father greeted me this Sunday morning with a smile: "Jeem, today we make some ice cream."

I took my little homemade wagon and brought home some free ice chips from the ice plant. In the meantime, my sisters Lia and Mary had made up the ice cream slurry and we were soon taking turns cranking our ice cream maker.

We were all gathered at the kitchen table eating our ice cream when father made his announcement. In his enthusiasm he spoke in Italian, telling us that he had bought some lots facing the nearby boulevard and that we were going to build a new home.

Andy and I were soon pressed into the simpler carpenter duties. We noticed that my father, with paintbrush in hand, was sprinkling the ends of our stack of lumber with red paint. When we asked him why, he just said that if we heard any hammering in the area to let him know. Evidently, someone had been stealing our lumber.

A few days later I did hear some hammering in the distance and I reported it to him. Without explanation but with a wry smile he said, "I feex 'em."

Our red-nosed Irish deputy sheriff, who was also a small-time political boss, would make his rounds to promote his favorite candidates and, of course, have several glasses of wine with the neighbors. This time my father requested a special favor from him, and the three of us went to investigate the source of the hammering which I had heard.

We approached the man who had a saw in hand.

"I want to see your construction, sir," our sheriff demanded in a gruff, intimidating voice. Sure enough, there was the lumber that my father had sprinkled with red paint!

At first there were denials, then pleadings, and finally an offer to pay for the stolen lumber.

"How about it, Gigi?" the deputy sheriff asked my father. "It sounds fair enough to me."

"No-sir-ree," was my father's reply. "I want every piece of wood back to where it came from—and the same way it was taken."

"But some of it is sawed and nailed into this barn," the sheriff reasoned.

My father was adamant and he repeated his demands slowly and firmly.

"Okay," the sheriff said finally, "Take all the lumber back or I will have to report you."

The neighborhood was treated to an amusing sight as everyone watched two men trudging over the Southern Pacific tracks for several days, returning both new and used lumber back to its origin. It was shortly thereafter that their disgrace forced them to move from the area.

"Boys, you don't have to be afraid of the creek any more," said father.

Could it be that the lumber thieves and the masked men were one and the same? Andy and I were sure of this when we went to get mother's bean poles at the creek. We found a large hole that had been dug out amongst the willow trees. Here were the remnants of a bootlegger's whisky still!

Ambrose Strikes Again

THE LARGE TWO-STORY FRAME BUILDING had a commanding view of its surroundings: a scattering of small homes that increased in density as they extended toward the center of town. On the other side were opens fields and the high railroad grade that shielded our neighborhood. On the street side, near the apex of its roofline, appeared bold, raised lettering: PERES SCHOOL - 1904.

The entrances on both ends of the building were identical, each having a broad open stairway, a generous landing, and more steps to a roofed-over portico. The two playgrounds were separated by a sheltered but divided rustic runway that intersected a long structure containing the somewhat primitive toilets. The primary grade school yard was further bordered by a long L-shaped, one-story building that housed the classrooms. A number of large acacia trees completed its boundaries.

School assemblies were held in front of the stairway. The landing was the stage and the chorus stood on the stairs. On very special occasions we primary graders were marched around to the upper grade side. We stood at attention through all the patriotic songs and speeches. The speeches we did not understand and the Star Spangled Banner was beyond our vocal range. It did not matter, as we were awed by all the flags, bunting and decorated breasts of the uniformed soldiers of past wars, including the now-aging Spanish-American War veterans.

As a third grader I was fully conscious of my immigrant and rural background. Even on cold winter mornings I was careful to walk through the icy puddles of water in order to remove any remnants of barnyard droppings that might have clung to my rubber boots. I would silently rub my feet along the cast iron stand of my desk in order to ease the itching discomfort of the resulting chilblains.

I was proud of that desk—as if it were my very own. It was here that I could live in a world of fairy tale books, my imagination spurred by the Arthur Rackham illustrations. It was also here that I could feel equal to the "American" children in our arithmetic and writing exercises. With pen and ink in hand, we would scratch along with Miss Robinson's nasal sing-song chant, *"Swing up—down—around—over."* She was a true disciple of the Palmer method of arm-movement penmanship.

Recess was another matter, as I was sure that my hand-knitted black cotton stockings that were forever falling down from my faded corduroy knee pants were noticed by all. Lunch time was even worse as it revealed my embarrassing school lunch that was wrapped in my parents' foreign language newspaper. The apple was always well-impressed into the soggy scrambled egg sandwich. How I envied the other children with their neat lunch bags containing sandwiches of store-bought bread filled with meat cuts and pink jellies all wrapped in crisp wax paper. Strange, I thought, they don't eat the crusts of their bread. Aren't they ever hungry?

The boys from my neighborhood across the railroad grade usually played under the acacia trees. It was unpaved there so it provided the soft earth for games we liked to play, such as aggies, pug (marble games), or pee-wee. More importantly, we were shielded from the ever-watchful eyes of our fearsome principal, Old Biddy Haustler, whose office windows dominated the entire play area. Periodically she would stomp onto the portico in her high laced black shoes, her posture stiff but correct.

She was tall and her gray hair brushed up into an outmoded pompadour added to her intimidating height. From her well-corsetted black bodice she removed her pince-nez glasses, placed them on her aquiline nose and peered down on her domain. The clenched hand on her hip held the ever-present ruler, her scepter of enforceable authority. A slow, sweeping glance was all that was needed to quiet the cacophony of schoolyard sounds. Satisfied that all was under control, she would promptly pivot on the balls of

her feet and march back to the privacy of her office, unaware of the problems that might be generating in the shadows of the acacia trees—in the form of a small boy named Ambrose.

In the three years since Ambrose moved into our neighborhood I had become aware of the texture and form of the reputation he was shaping. His daring exploits were fun but the stature they gave him seemed to please him even more. He invented such games as warring with mud balls and fresh "horse apples," and when these were not in season he developed the game of "corker." It consisted of two participants punching each other in turn on the fleshy part of the shoulder. The rules were so fair and explicit they would have been the envy of the Marquis of Queensbury himself. Even feinting or flinching drew a disqualification. When the pain was too great for a contestant to bear, the contest was over. Many times it was ended by mutual consent. It never involved anger or the shame of defeat.

Ambrose would deliver his best blows with pretended casualness to indicate that he had much harder ones in reserve. He ignored the ones he received as though he was completely insensitive to pain. He eventually ran out of victims, but he never challenged me, nor I him, as we both sensed that it would lead to more serious matters.

I enjoyed Ambrose's company, however, and I was impressed by the confident way he seemed to sidestep the pitfalls of youth.

It was late one day after school when, under the acacias, Ambrose and I were comparing our marble winnings of the day.

"Have you got any kerosene at your house, Jim?"

"Sure, in the barn lanterns at home. Why?"

"Never mind. I'll give you a tau and a steely for it."

"No deal unless you tell me what's it for."

"Okay. Well, it's like this—I want to pull one off on those fancy town kids." He then went into the details of his plan that involved the ancient plumbing marvel that was housed in the long hut adjacent to our trees.

We entered the building and took care of our needs at the sheetmetal urinal whose flushing waters joined that of the open metal trough that ran under the seats of a long row of cubicles. We then went into the first cubicle and watched the slow current go by. Ambrose crumbled his homework paper and waited with paper poised. When the mysterious but periodic flush of water occurred he dropped it into the torrent. We dashed to the last cubicle just in time to see the flotsam disappear into the black void of the earthly beyond.

Satisfied with the results of our experiment, we sauntered homeward on the path that crossed the fields and the railroad. Ambrose paused at the top of the grade.

"Hey, I'll bet that a little of my old man's black gunpowder would spice it up a bit!"

Our minds visualized the scene and we laughed as we slid down the dry, grassy embankment.

Alone now with my after-school chores, I began to have second thoughts about the matter. Something was sure to go wrong. We would be caught. My whole unblemished record was at stake. It was all because of Ambrose, I thought, as I decanted the kerosene into a small flask...

▲ ▲ ▲

We were ready at recess time, but the cubicles were less than half occupied. Lunch time would be better. We saved our lunch wrappings and added them to the small bundle tied with string which we had hidden in the bushes that bordered the toilets. I waited in the first stall to secure its critical position.

"Not enough customers. Next recess for sure," was Ambrose's comment when the bell rang. We went back to our respective classrooms, his being half a grade lower than mine.

The day seemed unbearably long but the last recess of the day finally arrived. I again closeted myself in the first cubicle. This time the other stalls began to fill and Ambrose entered mine with his bundle. He had me hold it as he sprinkled it—first with kerosene and then with gunpowder. To my surprise he tucked a few small red cylinders into the mess. My gosh—*firecrackers!*

Ambrose struck a match and applied it with perfect timing. "Drop it in!" he commanded as he slipped away.

I, foolish me, was caught in the crush of boys at the exit door. My desperation gave way to a flash of brilliance. I dropped my pants to half mast and mingled with the victims as we made our way out to the open yard.

There stood Ambrose holding his side with laughter and pausing only to point a finger at me and then doubling over with laughter again.

The bell sounded and we were soon back in our classrooms again. My embarrassment mixed with anger continued as I detected the muffled giggles and sly glances of my classmates.

Sitting at my desk, I did not have full view of the play yard through the classroom windows, but I could see a gray whiff of smoke rising from the ventilators of the toilet building. Later, I heard the crunch of adult footsteps criss-crossing the graveled play yard. My pen splattered ink as I tried to follow Miss Robinson's lead.

▲ ▲ ▲

The school day was nearing its end when I saw Ambrose being escorted up the stairway to Miss Haustler's office. Miss Robinson's rhythmic chant continued as she inspected our efforts. She stopped by my desk and sniffed several times.

Damn, it's that kerosene smell on me! I concluded.

"James, come with me!" and I, too, was escorted across the yard and up the stairway to my impending doom.

In the gloomy hall was Ambrose, with his teacher and Miss Haustler. Before they could hustle me off into the office alone, Ambrose indicated to me, with a subtle sign to his pursed lips, that he had not squealed on me.

The steady tick-tock of the huge pendulum clock counted the long seconds as I awaited the verdict. Just two minutes before the school dismissal bell was to ring, the door opened and I was led from my holding cell. We all marched down to the landing and waited.

The bell sounded, releasing the children. Seeing us on the landing, they gathered about the stairway below.

"Ambrose," announced Miss Haustler in a high strident voice, "I am going to make an example of you.

"Hold out your hand," she demanded.

Ambrose did so, but the ruler cut through the air harmlessly as he withdrew it just at the last moment.

A calm smile crept over his otherwise expressionless face. The children tittered. The enraged woman glared and, taking Ambrose's hand by its fingertips, delivered several resounding smacks with the ruler. His smile and indifferent posture held.

Exasperated by now, the poor woman beat his hand in a growing frenzy, but this had no effect except for the rising murmur from the children below. Finally, our two teachers restrained her and the defeated old lady was led away. Never was she able to rule by the rod again.

Ambrose and I descended the stairway and the children parted in awed silence as we made our way across the yard to the drinking fountain. I held the valve as Ambrose drank deeply. He then let the cold water cascade over his red and swollen hand.

He looked up at me and his smile broke into a broad grin.

"*Je-sus*, Jim, it sure hurt like hell!"

All About Aeroplanes

LOOKING OVER THE GUNNER'S RIGHT SHOULDER one could see the Enfield machine gun spitting fire into the back of a helmeted enemy pilot whose arms were thrust upward as in a gesture of supplication. To the left a biplane plainly marked with an iron cross was in a smoking, spiraling dive. In the background, amongst the white flecks of clouds, other airplanes were engaged in the classic dogfights typical of World War I.

This scene, so vividly depicted on the cover of a precious pulp magazine belonging to my oldest brother William, was so emblazoned upon my mind that it has remained as my earliest recollection of war and airplanes. It was several years later, around 1920 and at the age of six, that I first saw an airplane in flight. It happened when I was occupied with some menial task, such as filling the woodbox for the kitchen stove, when I heard a sound coming from the sky. Then I saw it—a real airplane!

"An aeroplane! An aeroplane!" I shouted to no one in particular, "A real aeroplane!"

The fiery scene on the magazine cover was rekindled and although the war was but a vague memory in our young minds, we boys still chanted a WWI ditty in our mock war games:

"Kaiser Bill went up the hill to take a look at France,
Kaiser Bill came down the hill with bullets in his pants!"

In the years that followed, these sightings became more and more frequent but the children would stop whatever they were doing, run to an open area and then shout and wave their caps or shirts at the phenomena in the skies. No game—such as migs, pee-wee, or tin-can hockey—that we might have been engrossed in could match the excitement of watching the smoky sky-writing of a Lucky Strike cigarette ad.

One day, my friend Lou and I were squatted behind our barn, friction taping a discarded cracked bat and a coverless baseball, when we heard the approaching roar of a low-flying aircraft. We ran out into the field waving frantically, and this time we were rewarded for our efforts. After a slow turn, the pilot made a second pass at us and dipped his wings.

He waved back to us as he passed and we were in ecstasy as we watched the yellow plane dropping steadily and then disappearing over a clump of eucalyptus trees.

"I'll bet he's landing in the hay field near the crick!" shouted Lou as we started to chase after it. It was then that I first became aware of Lou's speed and stamina, in spite of his stocky build, and I struggled to match his stride. Then, emerging from a cornfield, we saw it—a bright yellow Jenny, with its motor still running, kicking up a cloud of dust. There were no runways, hangers, or even a barn, just a tent and a few bright pennants waving in a light breeze. Behind this line of flags was an assortment of motor vehicles and a scattering of people. This was the so-called "barnstorming" of the early twenties!

We retreated to the edge of the cornfield and, lying on our stomachs with our chins resting on the heels of our hands, we watched the proceedings intently. We focused on the leather-jacketed and helmeted pilot. He was dressed in army twill khaki breeches and shiny high-laced boots. His goggles were pushed back upon his forehead and a bright neckerchief flowed about his throat. Our minds absorbed detail after detail so, like the storage banks of a computer, the information would later be available for instant recall.

One of the bystanders approached the pilot and handed him some money as he was assisted into the two-seat, open-cockpit plane. The pilot revved his engine and tested his controls. An assistant pulled the chocks that were blocking the wheels. The engine roared and the prop kicked up a cloud of dust. The plane taxied about a bit to avoid a ground squirrel's mound and then the engine strained as it gained speed. With fists clenched and our stomachs taut, we strained with it until, after a bump or two, it lifted serenely. Making a long banking turn, it headed out over to the baylands. We watched until our view was blocked by the willows and poplars that lined a nearby creek.

"Sure wisht I could ride it, Jim."

"Yeh, me too."

"Mebbe when we're older and could earn some money."

"Wouldn't ya be *sceerd?*"

"Naw—well, some, I guess."

Thus we talked until, in less that twenty minutes, the plane returned to the field. The pilot shook hands with the passenger and then the whole process was repeated with another brave soul.

As the afternoon wore on, the small crowd thinned out as the people left in their various Hudsons, Essexes, Stars and Model T's. When the last customer left, the pilot helped his assistant in pulling up stakes and loading their flatbed truck with fuel drums, water jugs, ropes, tarps and other paraphernalia. We wanted to be close at hand and talk to them but we were too shy—or was it that we were so filled with wonderment that we needed time to digest it all? As they left, we emerged from the cornfield and waved our unnoticed goodbyes. We were alone in the summer setting sun—except for the ground squirrel who, by now, had recovered from his torment.

Removing our shirts, we bundled some of the ripening corn into them for our families—in order to soften any reprimands we might receive for having disappeared for so long. We slowly walked the road home as our bare feet sensuously enjoyed the thick, soft layer of still-warm earth.

▲ ▲ ▲

In the days that followed Lou and I engaged ourselves in a spate of construction. Neither of us had ever possessed store-bought toys and so it was only natural that our recent experience inspired us to transform that ever-present scrap wood pile into replicas of the little yellow airplane.

The planes we made ranged from "sit-in" types to hand-whittled models.

It was rare indeed when commercial toys were seen in the neighborhood. Such a case was when a visiting boy sported a pair of roller skates which he soon tired of as there was only one paved street in the area. These skates we soon converted into a pair of "racing coasters," requiring only a short length of two-by-four, a vertical "lug box," and two sticks for handlebars.

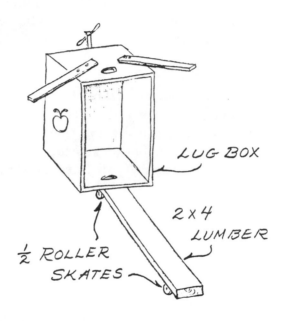

One windy day as we were "zooming" our hand-held airplane models, we discovered that the crudely fashioned, loosely-nailed propellers on our airplanes revolved. Our inventive minds and our creative hands were soon at work and it was not long before we had models mounted high above our backyard water tanks, swinging into the wind with propellers racing. All the boys in the area soon became engaged in the activity and the results got more sophisticated when a new source of material became available. It happened when a dining car porter tossed a crate from the transcontinental train as it was slowing down the grade just before

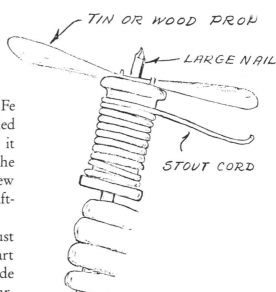

TIN OR WOOD PROP

LARGE NAIL

STOUT CORD

the Richmond Santa Fe terminal. We scrambled after the box wood as it came tumbling down the embankment, for we knew it would serve our aircraft-building purposes well.

Perhaps it was just thoughtfulness on the part of the porter that he made this drop a weekly occurrence, but I suspect he might have delighted in the furor he created just as some might enjoy the results of tossing a bone to a pack of hungry dogs.

Our interest in aircraft heightened even more when a new boy, Willie, moved in amongst us. Willie introduced us to what he called (if memory serves me accurately) a "gyroplane." The airborne portion was simply a flying propeller whose behavior was something between a boomerang and a modern frisbee. Its launching method was an ingenious if simple device, consisting solely of a large spool, a large nail, a piece of string and, oh yes, two small headless nails. A piece of tin was shaped and bent in the form of a propeller and two small holes were pierced at the hub. Using the perforated propeller as a template, the two small nails were driven into the spool astride its hole. The spool was wrapped with a length of stout string and the whole assembly was slipped over the pointed end of the big nail, which was held in the left hand. With an upward thrust of the left arm and a simultaneous pull of the string with the right hand, the tin propeller would whiz into the air, sailing and swerving in a fine, if unpredictable, flight.

We boy engineers learned to reduce some of the causes of erratic flight and were soon holding contests for height and distance.

Our favorite launching pad was off the railed platforms of our water tanks, which we learned to scale without fear. A fast slide down the water pipe was made by the loser who had to retrieve the props for the next try.

We found that larger spools and propellers made from heavier tin resulted in better performance. Unfortunately, this also resulted in a vicious cut over Willie's eye when one of my launchings misfired. The activity was immediately outlawed by our parents.

Willie did not discourage easily, however, and before his wound healed he presented us with a new flying device. It was a simpler one and much more danger-ous—just two plaster laths about a foot and a half long, securely nailed together at the middle in the form of a cross. The leading edges were whittled upward to provide the lift, as in a four-bladed propeller. It was  launched like a baseball pitcher throwing a sidearm curve. The results were fantastic—and just as erratic.

Inevitably, what with half a dozen boys slinging these missiles about, the shattering of windowpane glass was soon heard. I'm sure it was just a coincidence that Willie's family moved from the neighborhood shortly thereafter!

▲ ▲ ▲

It was these "little kid days" that Lou and I were reminiscing about as we sat astride a main steel beam of the Santa Fe trestle which spanned the Southern Pacific railroad tracks. Yes, we were older, perhaps about twelve or so, but really not old enough to hold down regular part-time jobs. Many Sunday afternoons found us with no "show money" and a bit lonely, but these railroad tracks sometimes presented us with a highway to adventure. We often talked a lot about our hopes and expectations but "growin' up" seemed to take an eternity as we were both anxious to "get going."

Unfortunately, sometimes these discussions degenerated into violent arguments over such small, mundane matters as the direction of True North or whether Los Angeles lay west or east of Due South. We were, of course, just exercising our debating skills, but to the uninitiated bystander—such as the old hobo ensconced under the trestle—it had a fearful impact.

The old fellow bravely rescued us from our precarious perch and remonstrated that it didn't really matter whether the little yellow airplane of our past childhood experience had wire or disk wheels. He insisted that we shake hands. Then, after "no-thanking" this kindly, bearded old man for a proffered sip of his coffee brewing in a tin can, we continued on our way, each balance-walking one of the rails in friendly competition.

Lou's keen sense of balance eventually discouraged me from this activity and I suggested that we check out the abandoned pear orchard up along the right-of-way.

However, we weren't the first to arrive. We found it was occupied by a band of gypsies indulging in a bit of curious festivities. From our vantage point on the railroad grade we could see into a partial clearing. They were roasting a small pig over an open fire. Somewhere amongst the tress an accordion and a violin gave forth with strange and exotic music. Soon there were tambourines and dancing. The women were dressed in colorful, long and full-flowing gowns and the men wore bright sashes about their waists. The music and dancing reached a crescendo and we feared for the little naked children that were underfoot. Our mothers had warned us about *Zingaros* and their proclivity for stealing young children, so we hurriedly moved on.

We passed by the small farms of the townships of Sunnyside and San Pablo and rested at the overpass at San Pablo Creek. I produced a squashed sandwich from my pocket—which my mother invariably wrapped in newspaper—and shared it with Lou.

Lou expressed some interest in the paper and that it was the back section of the *Oakland Tribune* instead of the usual *Voce del Populo* that our parents subscribed to. I explained that it was an "extra" from my older brother Andy's paper route. We divided the paper in half and perused its contents.

"Lookit here, Lou, a pusher-type model plane that can really fly! It says we can use balsa or sugar pine. What's balsa? It says to use Japanese tissue paper and banana oil and *a-cry-lic* glue. What are they?"

"We're goin' to need some dough," Lou summarized, but our minds went right to work trying to figure out what we could substitute for some of these special materials. We concluded, however, that we could have a much better chance of success if we had the money to purchase the particularly light materials.

The pungent odor of creosote emanating from the pile of railroad ties we had been sitting on did not seem to agree too well with the sandwich that was now in our stomachs, so we started back. I folded the plan for the pusher plane and put it in my pocket. Curiously, Lou did the same with his portion of the newspaper and I was about to ask him the reason when we were both startled by the clarion call of a trumpet and the rising shouts of a crowd of voices.

We left the tracks and moved through the trees in the direction of the noise. There it was—a new arena constructed of rough boards.

We cased the whole area trying to figure out how we could breach the enclosure. No chance, we decided. I wondered aloud how Ambrose, that clever boy who lived next door to me (and was our mutual nemesis) would have attacked such a problem.

"Heck, he'd just walk in like he owned the joint," said Lou depreciatingly.

"Well, why not? What have we got to lose?" I said, somewhat surprised at my own reaction. There was a period of tense waiting until the gate man was distracted by some late arrivals. We then sauntered through the gate.

"Hey, boys!" came the gateman's yell, but we split, darting under the bleachers and into the restless crowd, where we melted away.

We were entranced by the color and the fanfare and were caught up with the excitement of the crowd. The *picadores*, on their splendid padded horses, were impressive as they placed the darts on an enraged bull. The skill of the *banderilleros* as they placed their colorful staves into the bull's shoulders was unbelievable. But when the Matador performed with his cape, displaying such great courage as he went through one *veronica* after another—it was almost too much for us!

"I think he is going to kill the bull now!" exploded Lou in a voice that attracted the people about us.

"No," came the reply of a man beside us. "This is a *Portagee* bullfight. Can't kill 'em in California anyhow."

After a series of bulls were processed, we learned that a Portuguese association had promoted this affair as a climax for their Shamarita festival. The crowd was now leaving and we were making our way out when we were suddenly grasped from behind.

"Now you will pay!" said the gruff voice of the heavy-set and swarthy gatekeeper. "You have no money, eh? Now you can work it off, boys! Pick up every empty bottle in the stands—no, just the Cokes and the Nehis.

We did not mind the work and, in due time, we had a huge heap of bottles in their respective boxes.

"Well now, count them. No, never mind, I will count them by the boxes. Ten full Nehis and twelve Cokes, that's twelve to the box, that's—let me see—that's—"

"Two hundred and sixty-four," said Lou, who was quick with arithmetic, "and nine more makes two hundred and seventy-three."

The man scowled at this bit of upmanship, but he reached into his compartmentalized little canvas apron and began counting out money in the palm of his hand.

"Two, two-fifty, two-seventy and three." Was he paying us? we wondered.

"Two seventy-three," he said sternly as he handed Lou the money, "And, next time, ask—*don' sneek een!*"

▲ ▲ ▲

We ran back to the railroad track, saying nothing for awhile, just content with our adventure and good fortune.

"I'll bet we have enough money to buy all the stuff we need to make two pusher planes!" I volunteered.

"Pusher planes be darned! We're gonna fly in a *real* one. In Alameda—see here," said Lou, extracting that piece of newspaper he had placed in his pocket earlier. "It says we can ride an airplane for two dollars apiece. We'll need some more dough, though, and maybe two-bits apiece for car fare."

"Alameda? I've been to Alameda Seashore Park; my godfather took me there. Think we can really do it, Lou? Bring your stuff over. I'll see the junky Saturday. Gosh, maybe we can do it!"

As we passed by the Certainteed Linoleum Plant I broke off and made my way under a chain-link fence. Lou followed. We scratched through the small piles of wet pulp and metal tailings which were the clean-up dregs of the rag-stripping operations of the factory in their manufacture of "Congoleum." This messy stuff consisted of indigestible bits like corset snaps, buttons (including the campaign kind), bent safety pins, and paper clips. Occasionally we found bent coins, mostly dimes and pennies. Our net take was thirty-three cents, if we could straighten out the coins. Not much, but it would help!

I remembered that it was Ambrose who has shown me this trick. It brought to mind another of Ambrose's forays. Yes, the bank!

The next day we walked downtown. Even though the Seventh Street car line had been abandoned, we would not have considered paying the seven cents required for the mile run. At Tenth Street we stopped at the Mechanics Bank of Richmond—that is, at the back of the bank. Lou was posted as lookout and I, with a small square of wire mesh screen, sifted the lower cinders of the bank's incinerator. The result was only twenty-two cents, which meant we still had about a dollar to go. There were no new dumpings at the bathtub foundry (remember the cast-iron mining operations we boys had there?) so the ensuing days brought only a few pounds more to add to our junk collection. Friday, however, we hit upon a bonanza when Lou noticed the Pacific Gas and Electric Company was installing a new powerline. Much to the annoyance of the workmen, we hung around picking up short pieces of insulated copper wire. In order to get rid of us, the foreman gave us a coil of "short ends" and told us to "beat it!"

In no time at all we built a small bonfire and burned off the insulation on the wire. We did this because we didn't have much trust in the junkman's "estimates." We wanted to be paid for its net weight—by scale.

It was Saturday morning and at the usual call of *"Rags-bottles-sacks..."* there came an eager reply:

"Hey, Junky, over here!"

There was an unusual amount of sparring, questioning of scales, disagreement on the value of scrap copper, and the estimated weight of the scrap iron was challenged. When the junkman offered us eighty cents for the whole lot, I countered with one dollar and twenty cents, using one of his own phrases: "Take it or leave it."

"Ninety cents and I von't make a dime—so help me Got!"

I noticed Ambrose approaching from his blind side.

"One dollar-ten," was Lou's next move.

I shook my head negatively, more for the junkman's benefit than for Lou's.

"Okay, okay, one dollar even, and not a penny more. And you load it on the truck," he added, grumbling to himself.

"Good enough," said I, "if you let me crank your engine." His old one-horse rig had been replaced by a much-used second-hand Model T truck.

We loaded the stuff onto the truck, trying not to look at Ambrose, who was hidden in a crouch underneath.

The old junkman retarded the spark lever on the steering column while I positioned myself at the crank. The engine was still warm, so there was no need to pull the choke-wire which extended through the radiator. I carefully "palmed" the crank handle (without a thumb grip, to avoid injury in case the engine kicked back). With a single upward swing the engine started.

We watched as he slowly drove off. This time we were not a bit impressed with Ambrose who had stealthily mounted the back of the truck and was tossing off some scrap copper while the junkman sang his sleepy, "Rags, bottles, sacks..." We were ready for our flight!

▲ ▲ ▲

That night I hardly slept at all in anticipation of the next day. I pictured myself like a bird in lofty flight, slipping in and out amongst the soft, fluffy clouds and quietly indulging in the panorama below.

We skipped Sunday morning mass, which was rather rare for Lou, and mounted the streetcar for our destination. Just past El Cerrito, at a place called Stege Junction, we had to change cars and pay another fare, something we had not anticipated. The car proceeded along San Pablo Avenue which brought us into the heart of Oakland, after making what seemed to us a million stops and starts in the distinct towns of Albany, Berkeley and Emeryville. From there we somehow managed to make our way across the Oakland estuary and, by noon, we were at the "airport" (which, I believe, is now the Alameda Navy Supply Depot). The airport consisted mostly of one-story corrugated-iron buildings and we were directed to a very small one that resembled a roadside fruit stand. There were several pilots lolling about, sipping on soft drink bottles or just smoking and chatting. The scene was not too much different than the one we had witnessed at the cornfield years ago. The uniforms were similar and a little yellow plane near the stand appeared identical to the one we had seen before.

We stated our business when we finally got the attention of one of the pilots.

"Sure, fine," he said, "and that will be two dollars for each of you."

I nudged Lou as if to say, "I'll handle this one."

"Two dollars *EACH?*" I asked incredulously. It says right here that it's two dollars per ride," I insisted, pulling out the newspaper for proof. "We're little and don't weigh much—besides, we can both fit in one seat."

"Well—all—right," he said, with a wink at the other men. "Two bucks it is, and I'll give you kids a real ride."

He strapped us down in the forward seat and indicated to a friend that he was ready as he also strapped himself in and adjusted his goggles. The man reached high on the prop and gave it a yank—nothing happened. He reached again.

"Contact!" he shouted.

"Contact!" came the pilot's reply, and with a mighty pull of the prop the engine started.

The vibration and motor noise was something that I did not anticipate as we picked up speed down the runway. I knew we were airborne when the bumping stopped and my body became heavier as we made a steep climb. The wind in my face and the sound it made through the spars and guy wires did not help my composure. I glanced fearfully back at the pilot who returned my look with a smiling display of great white shining teeth.

Up we climbed and the earth tilted first this way then that way. I had no interest in the panorama, for my only thought was on survival.

Suddenly the earth was upside down as we went into barrel rolls and loops. I closed my eyes when the bottom seemed to drop out of the plane as we made a steep dive. I gradually opened them when I felt the pressure as we pulled out of it. I glanced at Lou as we leveled off. His face was white and he looked straight ahead as if in a trance. He didn't seem conscious of my presence.

It was comforting, though, that I was not alone in my fears. Gratefully, we welcomed our safe landing and we staggered back to the stand with the pilot between us. He patted our shoulders.

"Gutsy little fellers, these two," he remarked to his friends.

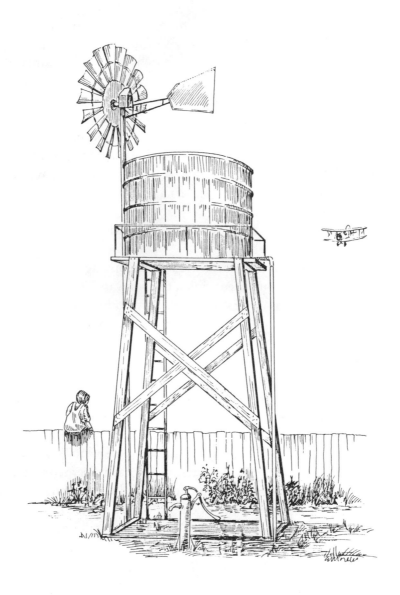

We managed a smile, but lost no time leaving the airport. The walk restored our equilibrium and it wasn't long before we were exchanging gibes at what each imagined the other had been going through.

Before boarding the streetcar home, we indulged in a bag of cookies we bought at a nearby small corner grocery store. The Mother's Cupcakes, Chocolate Nabiscos and Ladyfingers were washed down with lemon soda.

We then boarded the streetcar for home and read the car ads over and over again as the lurching and swaying of the car, coupled with its rattling and screeching of brakes, did not make for easy conversation. We were both feeling a bit giddy by the time we made the Stege Junction transfer and then, because of crowded conditions, we found ourselves in the stale atmosphere of the smoking section. It was all too much for us when we compared the color of green we wore on our faces!

We bolted for the rear platform and the conductor thought-fully put a couple of transfers in our pockets as we contained ourselves while waiting for the car to stop. With deep breaths of relief after disgorging our cookies, we lay in the grass for a period of recuperation. Somehow, in my mind, I visualized a sign that was on the rear platform whose meaning did not register at the time of stress. It was something about being "Unlawful to shoot rabbits from the rear platform."

I bolted upright. We had taken the wrong car! We then figured out that we were someplace between Richmond and Alvarado Park in San Pablo.

We decided to keep the transfers as souvenirs and we cut back across the fields for home. The long walk was salutary and when we came to within a block of my house, Lou called out—"Race you!" and we sprinted the rest of the way.

The last memory of that day was Lou continuing his run home, leaping over imaginary objects and broad-jumping over non-existing chasms. I can still hear his long "whoooo-wheeee," as he disappeared into the evening dusk.

Suzu

I SAW MY BROTHER ANDY leading our horse home with reins in hand. I also noticed that he had dirt and grass stains on his clothes.

"What happened, Ang?" Ang was short for his real name, Angelo. He was later called Andy.

"Prince and I were racing Carlo and his bay horse—had him beat until Prince tripped in a gopher hole."

Carlo was Ambrose's older brother. Carlo and Andy would race their horses bareback. They had no saddles as our horses were kept primarily for work duties, not for pleasure riding.

"We were up by the north creek bridge and saw some construction at the Japanese nursery. Carlo says we ought to go up there tomorrow to see if we can pick up some work."

The four of us arrived at the nursery the next day. The Japanese people were sitting as a group having tea and cookies. One young man arose and invited us to join them for tea.

"I'm Joe," he said, and introduced each person in turn, including a very pretty girl about my age named Suzu. We were not accustomed to tea but the cookies were a real treat. We were impressed by this family's friendliness.

"Ambrose, what's that thing hanging out of your back pocket?" asked Joe.

"It's a slingshot."

"What do you do with it?"

"I shoot birds with it. See these notches on the prongs?—one for each bird."

"How about that bird sitting on the ridge of the new glass hothouse?" grinned Joe in disbelief.

Ambrose did not reply. He placed a steel rivet in the slingshot's pocket and with deliberation pulled back, took aim, and let go. We were all prepared to hear the shattering of glass, but instead there was a dull thud and a fluff of feathers. While we all stared in disbelief Suzu ran and picked up the dead bird and cradled it in her hands. The accusing look she gave us all made us feel guilty. Suzu ran off with the bird without a word, but her actions were effective. I think that bird was Ambrose's last victim.

As if to change the subject, Joe asked us if we would like a few days work straightening up the nursery. Joe explained that he would not be around since he would be attending classes at the University of California. We respectfully thereafter referred to him as Joe College. We later learned that the nursery was in his name because his father, being an immigrant of Japan, could not own farmland according to the then-existing California laws.

Although Joe's father could speak fair English, Suzu in the next few days acted as an interpreter as she watched us work. We were nearing the end of our assignments and were tossing some used bricks into a pile. As I went to straighten up the pile my brother threw a brick which hit me on the side of my head. The corner of this brick made a bloody hole just past my left eyebrow.

Suzu was at my side in an instant. She took me in hand and lead me to her house. Her father, after giving me first aid, paid us all off for our labors. He then placed an envelope in my hand. We started home and I felt Suzu's soft little hand in mine as we walked along. Something was stirring inside of me that I had never felt before.

We reached the creek bridge. With a final squeeze of my hand and a special look in her eyes just for me, Suzu turned and hurried home.

"What's in the envelope?" asked Andy.

I opened it and found what was then a huge sum—in the form of a ten dollar bill.

"Gosh, I'd be glad to take a brick to the head for a ten dollar bill," said Carlo.

I'd be glad to take another one just to have Suzu hold my hand again! I said to myself.

Andy must have read my thoughts. "You know you can't marry a Japanese or Chinese in California—It's called the *anti-mis-seg-in-ation* law."

It didn't seem fair to me, but the *Examiner*, a Hearst paper, was constantly warning the public of the "yellow peril" in those days.

▲ ▲ ▲

Some fifteen years later I was courting my wife Esther. She and her girlfriend were about to embark on a cruise ship to Mexico for a vacation, and I thought I would surprise her with a "bon voyage" gift that she'd find in her stateroom after the liner left port.

I stopped in at a florist shop in town to make the arrangements. An attractive woman who waited on me assured me that the twelve red roses I bought would be aboard the ship. Then the young lady gave me a knowing look...

"Congratulations, Jim! I'm sure you will both be very happy." It was Suzu, the little girl I had met at the nursery as a young boy!

Shortly after her return from the trip to Mexico, Esther and I were married. Soon Japanese bombs fell on Pearl Harbor and Americans became involved in World War II. I often wondered how Suzu's gentle family fared during the war in the government internment camps set up for holding all the Japanese-Americans.

From Ambrose to Frank

IT WAS IN MR. MINOR'S junior high school gym class that I had the flu with its usual aches and pains. I was aware of his reputation of dealing severely with malingerers but I felt so poorly that I entered his office to be excused from "stripping," so that I could sit out the class activities. I began to recount my symptoms.

"What else? What else?" he demanded.

"My joints ache and..."

"I have just the medicine for you. Hold out your hand."

The paddle came down hard, but in shock and surprise I felt no pain. He repeated his prescription several times and I began to agonize. I did not protest. I finally turned my back to him and left the school. I slowly walked the long mile home. I felt degraded.

At least he didn't make me expose my ass for the paddling like he made some kids do, I said to myself. *That bastard.* But there must be a reason he doesn't like me—or at least doesn't trust me...

I'll get over this damn flu in time and I will go back to that monstrous school with its dark, dingy halls, and yelling, stinking kids. Well, at least my grades are okay, I thought as I tried to console myself.

It was not just because of the feeling of shame that I didn't consider mentioning the affair to my parents or even to my older brother. We were expected to work out our own personal problems.

The rest of the semester was uneventful and I managed to acclimate myself to a great degree to the institution-like process of a large school.

The early after-school hours were often free and the boys in our neighborhood got together for fun projects or games. We built crystal set radios from Quaker Oats boxes, flew our homemade kites and, on non-windy days, our rubber band powered airplanes.

Ambrose, my closest neighbor kid, usually spearheaded our activities, especially the competitive ones like slingshot contests. We'd often meet at his house because his basement was like a trading post. He possessed much of what we needed or treasured. It was here that we swapped bicycle parts, cart wheels and the like, which were often resourced at the city dump. Ambrose had quite an inventory on hand as he was a master at "horsetrading."

We boys were always competitive—especially Ambrose and me. We often resorted to ingenious tricks in order to outdo each other. Ambrose had found a pile of matched steel rivets for his slingshot at the defunct Western Pipe and Steel Works. No sparrow was safe from his increased ballistic accuracy. When we finally found his source of ammunition, he managed to direct our attention to a different activity. In this case, I evened the score by learning to cold forge arrowheads from copper tubing. My balanced arrows gave me quite an edge with our homemade archery equipment. When the rest of the boys got the hang of it, all the local real estate signs were soon reduced to sieves. It was natural for Ambrose and me to captain our teams in baseball or tin can hockey, but we both avoided any direct confrontation like wrestling—even in fun.

It was the last day of school before summer vacation. I was checking in some play yard equipment when the ball attendant presented me with a large carton.

"What's this for?"

"I don't know. Mr. Minor just told me to give it to you."

I started to open the box and saw that inside was an almost new set of boxing gloves. I bristled and closed the box quickly.

Maybe he thinks I'm a sissy and these will make a man out of me, was my first reaction.

Then... no, it's not that. He may feel bad about that licking he gave me. Perhaps he's not such a bad guy...just made a mistake is all. Well, it doesn't matter—but I'm sure going to learn how to use these damn things. Might come in handy someday.

My older brother Andy soon took possession of the gloves. Our basement became the boxing center of the neighborhood for the boys his age. I watched intently and observed their different styles. Some fought upright and some bobbed and weaved. I noticed that some were aggressive while others were content to be counter-punchers.

Andy was the boxer type. He would give me a lesson now and then, but in spite of the large training gloves all I would get from the lesson was a bloody nose.

"You ought to box with kids your own size," he suggested, "like Lou, Petro or Barney or..." he hesitated, "or Ambrose."

I shrugged my shoulders and didn't answer, but just the thought of boxing Ambrose caused my pulse to quicken. By now Ambrose had the reputation of being the bare-knuckle champion of our side of town.

It's those damn long arms of his that makes him so good at things like slamming home runs or — I winced at the thought — like landing those haymaker punches of his.

I began to lose interest in boxing, but a school pep rally boxing match or a championship fight broadcast on our Atwater-Kent radio would revive it. My heart would pound fiercely as if I were one of the contestants.

I generally sided with the boxer type, but slugger Jack Dempsey became my hero when he fought and beat Louis Firpo. It hurt me when Gene Tunney, with his boxing style, took Dempsey's measure.

By the time I was in high school the boxing gloves that were stored in our basement were beginning to grow a green mold on them. Lou was now our varsity fullback and Ambrose was on the school baseball team. The neighborhood boys were drifting apart and I had but a few friends in school. Lou, Ambrose and I had different classes but we occasionally ate our sack lunches together.

"Why don't you go out for football, Jim?" suggested Lou.

"Don't know the game."

"How about the line?"

"I'm too small."

"I'll bet you would make a good running guard—and don't tell me you can't stay after school because you have to work."

I did not use that excuse because I knew that his family had moved to a full-time truck farm and he still found time for after school sports.

"Okay. Maybe I'll try out for the 'B' squad."

I did just that and found myself, a 145-pounder, suited up in a harness fit for a 200-pound tackle. But it was fun.

To hell with after-school work, I told myself. Go out for varsity—get a decent football suit and play ball!

By spring practice I had picked up another five pounds. The coach and players seemed to respect my efforts and never made references to my size.

I was beginning to make friends, mostly football friends. We did things and went places, like ditching school to play in an unseasonable snow on Mount Diablo. I delighted in our friendly horseplay. It was good for me. Mr. Minor turned up at one of our practice sessions.

"Nice going, Jim," he said to me later. I was surprised but very pleased that he remembered me.

Just after the last varsity spring practice our coach let me know that I was due for one of the new suits he was ordering for the fall football season.

I felt good walking home from school that day. As I emerged from he path that wound through the hayfields, I spotted Ambrose and some of our old gang up on the Santa Fe railroad grade. They were waiting for me.

"How about a game of baseball, Jim?" Ambrose asked in a friendly manner.

"Sure," I said. It would be like old times, I thought, as we picked up a few more boys along the way.

We all went over to Ambrose's place. He came out of his basement with an assortment of gloves, balls and bats.

"One-a-cat or Two-a-cat?" I asked Ambrose.

"No, we'll choose teams and toss a bat for first ups. You toss, Jim."

"No, you toss, Am," I said. I, too, had learned to catch the bat handle in the right place to give our team "first ups," in the ensuing hand-grip-over-hand-grip decision.

Over the years we had developed a flexible game to suit the number of players on hand. Dry cow flops served well enough for base bags. Ambrose was the pitcher of his team and I could feel his frustration as we batted around our lineup several times. His team finally got the allotted three "outs" on us and we were due to take the field.

"Where is your glove?" I asked Ambrose who, I knew, had folded it and tucked it into his back pocket.

"You can't use it. You will bring it bad luck."

"Oh, that's silly kid's stuff," I countered.

"No dice...and maybe it's time we settle something else." He seemed to be assuming a fighter's stance.

"What in the hell are you talking about, Am?"

"It's now or never."

"You got to be kidding—" I felt a firm hand slap across my face.

I laughed in discomfort at his fair warning, but not for long. I saw his roundhouse right coming. I ducked, but not soon enough. The blow caught me high on the head and I staggered backward. *This guy really means business!*

He came at me now with both hands swinging. I crouched and tried to cover up but I took more blows to the head. In close, I managed a hard right to his midsection that made him grunt. I followed it up with a good left hook and then slipped away. We circled each other and my head began to clear.

Box! Box! I told myself.

He came at me again. I counter-punched with a series of short lefts and rights that made him back off.

Well at least I can get a few in before he finishes me...

He hauled back, telegraphing his right, and I stepped in with my right to his face. We clinched momentarily. We broke just as though we were in a boxing ring and a referee had parted us.

I bobbed and weaved. *Maybe I can last out until someone stops this damn thing—*

I tried a left jab. It worked and I began to realize that I was a bit faster with my punches than he was, and also that I was getting to him.

I was about to remind myself not to get careless when he caught me with a "good one," and he knew it. He then rained blows from every direction as though to end it all then and there. It was all I could do to cover up and try to survive the onslaught. We were both breathing heavily.

We broke again. My left jab landed and I followed it with a short right and left combination.

He doesn't seem to protect himself very well—he may be getting tired...

We came at each other again and again with much the same results. I knew I had him now, and I seemed to be getting my second wind.

I became aware of the crowd around us. There were no adults there. The boys were silent and their expressions seemed frozen. Their bodies cast still shadows in the late afternoon sun.

Why the hell doesn't someone come and stop this thing? I can't... Ambrose just keeps coming in for more and more punishment. Christ, what guts!

I saw Petro's mother on her back porch yelling and shaking her hands at us. I also saw Mr. Freeman, known by all as a pious man, climb his fence to get a better view.

"Damn them," I said to myself as my fists continued to do their devastating work, "*—and damn me, too.*"

I dropped my hands to my sides and my body began to tremble a bit. It was then that I heard and welcomed those softly spoken words from Ambrose:

"Jim, I think we have had enough." He put his hand on my shoulder. "Come over to my place and wash up."

He stroked the water pump handle while I washed, then we reversed roles.

"Guess I'll miss some school," he said flatly. I started to protest even though I knew he probably would.

"And I think I'll change my name from Ambrose to Frank."

His late father's name was Frank.

"It's my middle name, you know."

"Okay, Am...I mean, Frank."

We did not shake hands. We felt no need to. For the first time in all the years we spent growing up together we felt very close.

"I guess that's it," is all he said.

"Yeah, I guess," was all I could manage, and then I took the short path home.

Yes, I sure did lick him. I didn't break him, though. I don't think anyone or anything ever will.

That's the way I wanted it, I suppose. It felt strange knowing we were somehow no longer children, and that we would go our separate ways as men.

I felt I had lost something, too.

Epilogue

THEY ARE ALL GONE—the people who lived in the Iron Triangle. So are their houses, barns and gardens. Gone forever are the sounds of children at play, the clanking of the wine presses, and the banter of men at the bacci ball court.

Indeed, even the swimming hole where we boys splashed and laughed exists no longer. The Indian mound upon which the huge Holstein serving bull pawed the ground has disappeared, just as had its builders.

No longer are there meadows with the cry of the killdeer or the call of the lark. All gone in a flash of geological time—less than fifty years.

Although the borders of this community were well-defined, at that time it actually had no name. In my youth, however, the Iron Triangle was the center of my universe, my whole world.

I have not written these stories to place some symbolic wreath for its death. The early immigrant families that lived there would not have wanted it so. Instead, they welcomed the bulldozers, the paved streets, the modern commercial buildings, and even the freeways, all of which their energy and ambitions helped create. In their minds, this was a way of providing a better world for their children.

Let these stories be a remembrance, then, of their aspirations and their achievements.